RUBY the COPYCAT

by
Peggy Rathmann

SCHOLASTIC INC.

New York   Toronto   London   Auckland   Sydney

ISBN 0-590-43748-8

3 4 5 6 7 8 9 10   09   00 99 98 97 96 95 94 93

Printed in the U.S.A.

And at noon, Ruby and Angela hopped home for lunch.

Miss Hart turned on the tape player and said,
"Follow the leader! Do the Ruby Hop!"
So Ruby led the class around the room,
while everyone copied *her*.

The class cheered and clapped their hands
to the beat of Ruby's feet. Ruby was the best
hopper they had ever seen.

She hopped sideways with both eyes shut.

Ruby sprang from her desk.

She hopped forward.

She hopped backward.

The class giggled.
Ruby's ears turned red.
"But I did! I hopped around the picnic table ten times!" Ruby looked around the room. "Watch!"

Ruby peeled off a fingernail.

"I hopped," said Ruby.

Miss Hart folded her hands
and looked very serious.
"Ruby, dear," said Miss Hart
gently, "did you do anything else
this weekend?"

On Monday morning, Miss Hart said, "I hope everyone had a pleasant weekend. I did! I went to the opera." Miss Hart looked around the room. "Does anyone have something to share?"

Ruby waved her hand. Glued to every finger was a pink plastic fingernail.

"I went to the opera, too!" said Ruby.

"She did not!" whispered Angela.

Miss Hart smiled at Ruby. Ruby smiled at
Miss Hart's beautiful, polished fingernails.
"Have a nice weekend," said Miss Hart.
"Have a nice weekend," said Ruby.

Miss Hart closed the door of the schoolroom
and sat on the edge of Ruby's desk.

"Ruby, dear," she said gently, "you don't need to
copy everything Angela does. You can be anything
you want to be, but be Ruby first. I like Ruby."

Angela scribbled something on a piece of paper.
She passed it to Ruby.

The note said:

YOU COPIED ME!
I'M TELLING MISS HART!
P.S. I HATE YOUR HAIR THAT WAY.

Ruby buried her chin in the collar of her blouse. A
big tear rolled down her nose and plopped onto the note.

When the bell rang, Miss Hart sent everyone home
except Ruby.

Ruby smiled at the back of Angela's head.
Someone whispered. Ruby sat down.
"What a coincidence," murmured Miss Hart.

Ruby stood and recited slowly:

I had a nice pet,
Who I never met,
Because it always stayed behind me.
And I'm sure it was a cat, too.

Angela raised her hand. She stood by her desk and read:

I had a cat I could not see,
Because it stayed in back of me.
It was a very loyal pet—
It's sad we never really met.

"That was very good!" said Miss Hart. "Now, who's next?" Miss Hart looked around the room. "Ruby?"

On Friday afternoon, Miss Hart asked everyone to write a short poem.

"Who would like to read first?" asked Miss Hart.

When Angela came back to school,
she was wearing black.

By coincidence, on Friday morning, both girls wore red-and-lavender-striped dresses.

At lunchtime, Angela raced home.

On Thursday morning, during Sharing Time,
Angela modeled the flower girl dress
she wore at her sister's wedding.

Ruby modeled her flower girl dress, too,
right after lunch.

Angela didn't whisper anything.

On Wednesday, Angela wore a hand-painted
T-shirt with matching sneakers.

After lunch, Ruby hopped back to school wearing
a hand-painted T-shirt with matching sneakers.

"Why are you sitting like that?" whispered Angela.

"Wet paint," said Ruby.

When Ruby came back to school after lunch,
she was wearing a sweater with daisies on it.
"I like your sweater," whispered Angela.
"I like yours, too," whispered Ruby.

On Tuesday morning, Angela wore a sweater with daisies on it.

At lunchtime, Ruby hopped home sideways.

When Ruby came back to school,
she was wearing a red bow in her hair.
She slid into her seat behind Angela.
    "I like your bow," whispered Angela.
    "I like yours, too," whispered Ruby.
    "Class, please take out your math books,"
said Miss Hart.

At lunchtime, Ruby hopped all the way home on one foot.

Ruby raised her hand halfway. "I was the flower girl at my sister's wedding, too."

"What a coincidence!" said Miss Hart.

Angela turned and smiled at Ruby.

Ruby smiled at the top of Angela's head.

"Class, please take out your reading books," said Miss Hart.

"I hope everyone had a pleasant weekend," said
Miss Hart. "Does anyone have something to share?"

"I was the flower girl at my sister's wedding,"
said Angela.

"That's exciting," said Miss Hart.

Monday was Ruby's first day in Miss Hart's class.

"Class, this is Ruby," announced Miss Hart.
"Ruby, you may use the empty desk behind Angela.
Angela is the girl with the pretty red bow in her hair."

Angela smiled at Ruby.

Ruby smiled at Angela's bow and tiptoed
to her seat.

For Grammy Joy and Papa George,
who always try to set a good example.

Special thanks to Loma Vista School and
Pierpont School of Ventura.